MY LiFe
as a
toasted
Time Traveler

BOOKS BY BILL MYERS

Children's Series
McGee and Me! (12 books)

The Incredible Worlds of Wally McDoogle:
—*My Life As a Smashed Burrito with Extra Hot Sauce*
—*My Life As Alien Monster Bait*
—*My Life As a Broken Bungee Cord*
—*My Life As Crocodile Junk Food*
—*My Life As Dinosaur Dental Floss*
—*My Life As a Torpedo Test Target*
—*My Life As a Human Hockey Puck*
—*My Life As an Afterthought Astronaut*
—*My Life As Reindeer Road Kill*
—*My Life As a Toasted Time Traveler*
—*My Life As Polluted Pond Scum*

Fantasy Series
Journeys to Fayrah:
—*The Portal*
—*The Experiment*
—*The Whirlwind*
—*The Tablet*

Teen Series
Forbidden Doors:
—*The Society*
—*The Deceived*
—*The Spell*
—*The Haunting*
—*The Guardian*
—*The Encounter*

Adult Books
Christ B.C.
Blood of Heaven

the incredible worlds of **Wally McDoogle**

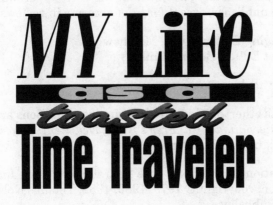

MY LiFe
as a
toasted
Time Traveler

Sullivan County Public Library

B I L L   M Y E R S

WORD
Kids!®
WORD PUBLISHING
Dallas·London·Vancouver·Melbourne

MY LIFE AS A TOASTED TIME TRAVELER

Managing Editor: Laura Minchew
Project Editor: Beverly Phillips

Cover art by Jonathan Gregerson.

Unless otherwise indicated, Scripture quotations are from
the *International Children's Bible, New Century Version*,
copyright © 1983, 1986, 1988.

Quotations marked NKJV are from the New King James
Version, copyright © 1979, 1980, 1982, Thomas Nelson,
Inc., Publisher.

Library of Congress Cataloging-in-Publication Data

Myers, Bill, 1953–
    My life as a toasted time traveler / Bill Myers.
      p.   cm. — (The incredible worlds of Wally McDoogle ; bk. #10)
    "Word kids!"
    Summary: After a future version of himself travels back in
time to warn Wally of an upcoming accident, he is confronted by
multiple future Wallys arguing that he must not try to rewrite
God's plan for his life.
    ISBN 0–8499–3867–8 (pbk.)
    [1. Time travel—Fiction. 2. Christian life—Fiction.
  3. Humorous stories.] I. Title. II. Series: Myers, Bill, 1953–
  Incredible worlds of Wally McDoogle ; #10.
  PZ7.M98234Mym   1996
  [Fic]—dc20   96–10293
                                                    CIP
                                                    AC

Printed in the United States of America

96 97 98 99 00   QBP   9 8 7 6 5 4

For Bill Burnett—
as you continue being an example
and setting the standard.

Trust in the Lord with all your heart,
And lean not on your own understanding;
In all your ways acknowledge Him.
And He shall direct your paths.

—Proverbs 3:5–6 (NKJV)

Contents

Contents

Chapter 1

Just for Starters...

The next time I try to do things my way instead of God's way, just shove a burning stick of dynamite into my hand, or push me off the World Trade Center without a parachute, or make me eat my little sister's cooking. Anything would be better than the pain of trying to run the show my way.

At least that's what I know now. Unfortunately, what I know now isn't the same as what I thought I knew then.

Confused? Me, too. So what else is new? Maybe I'd better start at the beginning. . . .

It all started with the Little League All-City Championship. I was playing for the Norton Lumber Knuckleheads. We were supposed to be the Norton Lumber *Knights*, but Coach thought *Knuckleheads* was a more appropriate name. You'd like Coach. He's always so kind and encouraging:

"All right, you knuckleheads," he shouted into the dugout. "We're one run ahead. If you can actually stop them from scoring this inning, we'll be All-City Champs. Now get out there and try not to make total fools of yourselves."

See what I mean? But he wasn't done yet.

"Oh yeah, and McDoogle, you're playing center field."

My jaw dropped to the dugout floor. Coach had kept me on the bench the entire game. Actually, the entire season. I didn't hold it against him. We had terrific players, and he expected each of us to do our part. My part, of course, was to go nowhere near the playing field when the game was in progress and, of course, to stay out of everybody's way. I had always succeeded in this mission . . . except for one time, just a few minutes earlier.

I had returned from the snack stand with my second Gooey Chewy bar of the game. I love Gooey Chewy bars. In fact, I'd eat them morning, noon, and night if it weren't for Mom and this thing she has about nutrition. Then, of course, there are those minor irritations like cavities, humongous dentist bills, and shouting dads.

Anyway, there I was, innocently chewing on a Gooey Chewy bar in the dugout when I accidentally tripped over a baseball bat. No problem, except for the part where I went flying into the air and landed on top of Phinnies Dooberslurp, our center fielder.

Fortunately, Phinnies broke my fall. Unfortunately, I broke his arm. In about three places.

But that was only the beginning of the fun and games. In my never-ending quest to be the greatest Walking Disaster Area of all time, Phinnies and I continued our little falling routine until we crashed down onto the end of the players' bench.

No problem, again, except Phinnies weighed just under three tons, which propelled the other end of the bench into the air like a jet-powered teetertotter.

Even that wouldn't have been so bad, if it weren't for the three reserve players sitting on that other end. The ones who were suddenly launched into the air like space shuttle astronauts. They might have made it into orbit, too, if they hadn't smashed into the dugout roof.

After the ambulance came and carted them off, Coach discovered we only had eight players left. Well, nine, if you count me. But we know better than to do that, right?

Well, we may know better, but Coach didn't. Apparently he wasn't as familiar with my world-famous klutziness as he should have been.

So, as everyone ran onto the field, I stayed

behind, explaining to him that it would be better
to play one player short than to send me out.

"The rules say I gotta let you play," he growled.

"But—"

"We'll be okay," he said, "just as long as you don't
move or blink. I don't even want to see you breath-
ing. Got that?" He towered above me, a mountain
of intimidation. "If you make the tiniest error,
McDoogle, so help me I'm going to boot you all the
way to Antarctica."

I guess he had heard of my reputation after all.
And since Antarctica is a terrible place to visit this
time of year, I figured it was best to obey him. I
headed out to center field and stood perfectly still,
not moving, not blinking, and just basically doing
my best imitation of not being there.

Our right fielder, Billy Buckleman, a great guy
and an even greater athlete, called over to me.
"Hey, Wally. Pssst, Wally."

"Yeah?" I whispered.

"What's with the glove?"

I glanced down at my mitt. From the looks of
things, I guessed I had it on the wrong hand. "Oh,"
I said, quickly switching it, "thanks."

"No, no," he laughed. "It's not the hand you're
wearing it on, it's how you're wearing it."

"What's wrong with the way I'm wearing it?"

"You've got it on backwards."

I glanced down again.

"How do you expect to catch anything with the BACK of your glove?"

He had a point. Then again, how did I expect to catch anything with the *front?* It's not that I'm unathletic, but last year they even cut me from the girl's knitting team. (Something about not trusting me to hold all those sharp, pointy, knitting needles.)

"Oh, and one final thing," he said. "Watch out for all the gopher holes out here."

I glanced around. He was right, there were a half dozen of the little critter's holes scattered about the outfield.

"Thanks," I said.

Jimmy Riordan, our star pitcher, stepped up to the mound. Six pitches and six strikes later he had retired the first two batters.

The crowd was going wild. One more out and we were going to be All-City Champs.

Unfortunately, the next batter hit a double. It should have been another out, but our third baseman, Thadius Snodgrass III, was too busy straightening the crease his mother had ironed down the middle of his baseball uniform to notice the ball rolling past him. By the time he finally got around to seeing it, the runner was on second base.

Coach was furious, screaming the same promises

to Thadius he had made to me about that free Antarctica vacation, courtesy of Boot-in-the-Pants Airlines.

Now things were tense. The tying run was on second, and the winning run was stepping up to the plate. It was Gary the Gorilla, the only seventh grader in the world who had a five o'clock shadow by high noon.

He took a couple of practice swings and waited.

Jimmy Riordan wiped the sweat from his face. He started his windup, checked second, then threw a smoking fastball right across the plate. Gary missed, swinging so hard that it was all the infielders could do to keep their hats from blowing off in the wind.

Jimmy went into his wind-up and fired a second pitch.

Another miss.

Another hurricane.

Now we were down to one last pitch. One last pitch and the title would be ours.

Jimmy started his wind-up, checked second, and threw another sizzler. But this time Gary caught a piece of it. The ball looped slowly into the air. An easy fly ball, another out . . . except for one minor problem.

You guessed it. It was heading directly toward me.

Now it was time to put aside my fears and face them like a man. It was time to stand up and become the true sports hero I knew I was. It was time to scream my head off:

"SOMEBODY, HELP ME!"

"I'm right here!" It was Billy. He was running toward me as fast as he could. "I've got it! I've got it!"

"Let him catch it!" Coach was shouting. "Let Billy catch it!"

I nodded my head, but the weirdest thing happened. Even though I was nodding my head yes, I was hearing my voice shout, "NO!"

Weirder still, it was my voice, but it wasn't coming from my mouth.

I spun around searching, trying to find out where the voice was coming from, when I noticed something even more unusual. Everything was now moving in super-slow motion. . . .

Coach was yelling at me, but it took him forever to get out the words.

Billy was running toward me, but it was doubtful he'd be arriving until Christmas of the year 2043.

And the ball?

I jerked my head up. It was still in the air but floating toward me very, very slowly.

And then I saw him . . . hovering about fifteen

feet behind me. There were all sorts of lights and sparks around him, and they all seemed to come from what looked like a portable vacuum cleaner strapped to his back. Then, of course, there was the toaster he had tied to his head. A toaster that had more smoke and fire shooting from it than our barbecue grill the last time Dad tried using it.

Oh, and there was one other detail. Although he was a bit older and taller, he looked exactly like me. Same dork-oid expression, same dork-oid clothes, even the same dork-oid glasses.

"Who are you?" I shouted. "What are you doing?"

"I've come to make you a hero."

"What are you talking about? Who are you?" I repeated.

"Wally Ulysses McDoogle, at your service."

"You can't be," I shouted.

"Why not?"

"Because that's me."

"Exactly."

"So, who are you?"

"You."

"No way. I'm me, you're you."

"Exactly. But I'm also you and you're me."

"If you're me, what's that make me?"

"Me."

"I think I'm getting a headache."

"Me, too."

"Listen," I shouted, "I'd love to continue this little hallucination, but if you don't mind I need to put my imagination on hold and get back into the game."

"That's exactly why I've come."

"What are you talking about?"

"I've come from the future, Wally. I've come to warn you of an accident you're about to have. If you listen to me, we can change history. You'll never be a dork-oid again. I can make you a hero. You'll be rich, world famous, loved by mill—"

"Look, I really appreciate the offer, but as you can see I'm kinda busy with reality right now. Maybe you can swing by a little later when I have time for a real mental breakdown."

"Wally—"

"Run along now, go haunt somebody else."

He let out a sigh which I had to admit sounded a lot like one of my sighs and said, "All right, if that's what you want."

He pulled out what looked like an oversized TV remote, pressed a bunch of buttons, and suddenly everything was at normal speed again . . .

The screaming Coach.

The soaring ball.

The running Billy.

I tried my best to get out of Billy's way, but it

seemed no matter where I ran, that was the way
he ran. When I went to the left he'd go to the left.
When I went to the right, he'd go to the right.

"Look out," he shouted. "Look out!"

"I'm looking," I cried, "I'm looking!"

And then it happened. My foot caught one of
those world-famous gopher holes, and I started to
fall.

"AUGHHH!"

But being the friendly type that likes to share
my good fortune, I didn't just fall by myself, I managed to plow into Billy along the way—

"OOAFFF!"

—and drag him down with me.

"WALLY, LET GO OF . . ."

But that was all he said before we hit the ground.
A moment later something hard and round hit my
head. Something hard and round that felt an awful
lot like a baseball. Now, normally I would have
cried out in pain, but at that particular moment
I was too busy being knocked unconscious.

I'm guessing the lights out routine only lasted
a couple of seconds. Because when I came to, the
crowd was still groaning. And for good reason.

We were finished. We'd lost. The tie-scoring run
was crossing home plate, and Gary, the winning
run, was right behind. The great Knuckleheads
had lost by a single point. One lousy point.

And there was only one person to blame.

As I lay on my back, trying to move, trying to guess how many bones I'd broken, I could hear the crowd booing me and Coach doing more than his usual amount of screaming.

Then, suddenly, the guy with the vacuum on his back was hovering over me again. "See what I mean?" he shouted.

I tell you, for a daydream he was sure pushy.

"Just do what I say," he shouted. "Let me change history and this will all be different. Never again will you be Wally the Dork-oid. You'll be Wally the Hero."

I rolled over onto my stomach. The crowd was going crazy. I don't want to say they were angry, but even with my glasses cockeyed I could see the foam frothing from their mouths.

I looked over to Coach. He was racing toward me with all the compassion of a pit bull gone berserk. Call me a pessimist, but somehow I suspected he wasn't coming out to congratulate me.

"Just say the word and I can change all this," the older version of me kept shouting. "I promise I can make you a hero. You'll be loved by millions."

Now I have to admit it was a tough choice. Being hated by the world, plus enjoying Coach's wonderful, upcoming trip to Antarctica . . . or being loved by millions.

But since I was sure Mr. Flying Vacuum Cleaner with the identity crisis wasn't real, and since I'm allergic to penguins, I decided to give it a shot.

So, still lying on my back, I groaned. "Sure, whatever you say."

Instantly there was a loud:

> *SNAP . . .*
> > *ZIP . . .*
> > > *FLASH . . .*
> > > > *POP . . .*

Suddenly I was standing back in center field. Suddenly Gary the Gorilla was back at the plate. And suddenly he connected with the ball again, sending it high into the sky directly toward me.

I couldn't believe what was happening. Needless to say, this Wally wannabe with the vacuum cleaner and toaster helmet was starting to get my attention.

Chapter 2

The Plot Sickens

To quote another famous baseball player, "It was déjà vu all over again."

"SOMEBODY HELP ME!" That was me screaming for help.

"I've got it! I've got it!" That was Billy running toward me to catch the ball.

Even Coach was shouting the same words of encouragement. "Let him catch it! Let Billy catch it!"

Incredible. Everything was exactly as it had been . . . well, almost everything. There was one difference. This time I knew what was about to happen. This time I knew I was about to step in a gopher hole the size of the Grand Canyon.

I glanced down. Sure enough, there it was, just waiting to grab my foot and destroy any hopes of remaining a normal, living human being. But remembering what had happened the last time, I quickly side-stepped the hole and kept running. That was the good news.

The bad news was, when I looked back up I'd lost track of the ball . . . until everything went into super-slow motion and ol' Vacuum Cleaner Boy with the toaster top suddenly hovered behind me again.

"It's above you!" he shouted. "Raise your glove and take two steps to the left."

I looked over to Billy. He was running toward me in slow motion. "But that's exactly where *he's* running," I shouted. "We'll crash into each other again."

"I'll take care of him. Just take two steps!"

Reluctantly, I did what he said.

"Now raise your mitt."

I did.

"Perfect."

More smoke and light shot out of his vacuum cleaner as he zipped down to Billy's side. Before I could stop him, he gave my friend a hard shove.

"Hey," I shouted, "you can't—"

But he was already pressing the buttons on his remote control:

> *SNAP* . . .
>> *ZIP* . . .
>>> *FLASH* . . .
>>>> *POP* . . .

And once again, we were back in real time.

Before I knew what had happened, the ball landed in my mitt. It was incredible. I, Wally McDoogle, had just caught a ball. Talk about a miracle. I mean it was right up there with Moses and the parting of the Red Sea. Think of it, me, Wally Klutz-oid McDoogle, actually being athletic. Incredible.

Once again the crowd was going crazy. But instead of booing me, they were cheering. And once again Coach was running onto the field. But instead of a free trip to Antarctica, he raced out and started patting me on the back. Normally I would have appreciated the gesture, but it's hard to be appreciative when you're being pounded in to the ground like a fence post. (Coach obviously didn't know his own strength.)

"Way to go, McDoogle!" he shouted. "You gotta be the world's luckiest idiot."

Coming from Coach this was a major compliment, and I felt bad not being able to answer. But I figured he couldn't hear me anyway, not over all the noise of smashing cartiledge and snapping bones.

Yet, I barely noticed the pain. After all, we'd won. The Norton Lumber Knuckleheads had just become the All-City Champs! And I was the reason.

The rest of the team surrounded me and tried
to raise me up onto their shoulders. But after
dropping me a half dozen times (after all, I am
still Wally McDoogle and such things are still
expected), they settled for some good, hearty high
fives. Except for the broken wrists and fingers,
I was having the time of my life.

"Whey, Whoaally!" I looked over and saw my
best friend, Opera, cramming his fifty-seventh hot
dog into his mouth. He was grinning ear to ear—
not a pretty sight, particularly with the stream of
mustard escaping out of both corners of his mouth.
Yes sir, the boy definitely liked his junk food.
"Whay woo woh!" he shouted.

"Thanks," I shouted back.

"Wally, over here!"

I turned. There was a bright flash. It was Wall
Street, my other best friend, taking a picture.

"What's that for?" I shouted.

"Baseball cards. They'll make us a million." Wall
Street was fond of making money, especially when
it came to making it off me.

"Oh, and here." She tossed me a giant, econo-
sized Gooey Chewy bar. "The guy at the snack
stand knows how much you like these, so he asked
me to give it to you free of charge."

"Great!" I shouted, as I tore off the wrapper.

"Of course, there's a five dollar handling fee to me for bringing it over to you," she said.

"Of course," I said. "Just put it on my bill."

But even then, during all the celebrating, I was feeling just a little uneasy. I mean, all of this praise, all of this congratulations, even the free Gooey Chewy bar . . . for what? For something I didn't really deserve.

Like it or not, I had a conscience, and it was beginning to work overtime. It was beginning to make me feel just a little bit guilty. Until I looked over my shoulder and saw Billy pulling himself up off the ground.

Suddenly, I was feeling a lot guilty.

True, I'd won the game, but it wasn't right. It was almost like I'd cheated or something. Like life was supposed to go one way, but I broke the rules and made it go another.

Unfortunately, as we continued to celebrate, the feeling continued to grow. . . .

* * * * *

The rest of the day was pretty much the same . . . victory celebrations here, more Gooey Chewy bars there. But all the time, the guilt kept piling up.

After an autograph session (courtesy of Wall Street, who was piling up dough faster than Jed Clampett), I finally made it home and crawled into bed. It had been one exhausting day. And something was wrong, terribly wrong.

As I munched on another Gooey Chewy, I reached for ol' Betsy, my laptop computer. It was time to start up another one of my famous superhero stories.

Yes sir, nothing like a little fantasy to help me get a better grip on reality. . . .

It has been another long day for the fantastically frustrated and phenomenally UNfamous...Flame Boy.

Even as a little spark, he had wanted to be a major superhero. But with all the other heroes around who drive cool cars out of cool bat caves or fly about in capes and long underwear, there was just no need for Flame Boy's unique skills.

Oh sure, being made of flame is a lot of fun when friends use him to toast marshmallows or light Fourth of July sparklers....But just try entering a building without setting off the smoke alarms or holding some girl's hand without having to race her to the nearest emergency burn unit.

In short, Flame Boy isn't happy being who he is. In fact, this very moment he is thinking of drowning his sorrows in a tall glass of water, when suddenly the Flame Phone rings.

Crackle-crackle-crackle...
Crackle-crackle-crackle...

Quicker than you can say, "Uh-oh, here we go again," Flame Boy races across the room while grabbing a fire extinguisher to put out the burning carpet behind him. He picks up the phone and answers, "Hello?"

"Hello, Pizza Gut? This is the President speaking. I'd like to order 200 deluxe pizzas to go, please."

"Come on, who are you kidding?" Flame Boy says. "You aren't the President."

"I certainly am, at least that's the name stitched on my underwear. Anyway, I'm about to declare a national emergency. But before I close down the country I want to make sure I have enough pizzas to hold me over. Oh, and could you add extra anchovies, please?"

"A national emergency? What happened?"

"My archrival, the arch-anarchist Arctic Guy, has just escaped from Coldsom Prison."

"No," our hero gasps a fiery gasp.

"Yes," the President says, "and he has just taken the sun hostage. He will not let its rays strike the earth until we give him every dollar in our treasury and promise to get rid of all those *Brady Bunch* reruns."

"You can't do that."

"I know. What would we do without those heartwarming adventures of Marcia and all those little cuties? Listen, could we have extra cheese on those pizzas?"

"Mr. President, I'm afraid you have the wrong number. This isn't Pizza Gut, but I'm sure I can help."

"If you're not Pizza Gut, then who are you?"

"I'm the one and only..." he gives a dramatic pause, waiting for the usual dramatic superhero music. But alas and alack (whatever that means), he has not yet achieved superherohood. There is only silence—which he tries to cover by coughing a lot and clearing his throat. He tries again. "I am the one and only...Flame Boy!"

Still more silence.

"Who?" the President asks.

"Flame Boy. I'm kinda new. But don't worry, Sir, I'll save the day. And you won't have to miss a single episode of those Bradys."

"Great! 'Cause this afternoon the kids think Alice is tattling on them, and they give her the cold shoulder and—"

"I better be going, Sir."

"Oh right, and don't forget the extra cheese."

Quicker than you can ask, "Isn't it just a bit coincidental for the President to be calling our hero?" Flame Boy races for the door.

Outside it's worse than he fears. It is so cold joggers are sweating icicles, people are using ice picks on their hot chocolate, and a polar bear has broken out of the local zoo to raid K-Mart for gloves and thermal underwear.

Flame Boy looks up to the sky and immediately sees the reason. A giant glob of Sunscreen #85 is between the sun and Earth. It is totally blocking off

all rays to our planet. Not a bad idea
for those afraid of getting a sunburn,
but a lousy idea for those not wanting
to freeze to death.

But how can our superkid reach the
giant blob of Sunscreen? How can he
save the world when he doesn't have all
the cool superhero gizmos that all the
other cool superheroes use and try to
dump on poor unsuspecting kids during
all those Saturday morning commercials?

Then he sees it, the unemployment
agency. And standing in line is a fire-
eater who hasn't had a job since the
last time the circus came through.
Quicker than you can say, "And I
thought the President calling him was
a bit much," our hero races up to the
fire-eater and convinces him to include
him in his act.

Grateful for a partner, the fire-eater
swallows Flame Boy's flames and spits
him high into the air toward the
Sunscreen #85. It is a beautiful sight
as Flame Boy shoots higher and higher
and higher some more.

But what will happen when he arrives?
Will he meet the sinister Arctic Guy?

Will he be able to dissolve the Sunscreen? And most importantly, will there be any more far-fetched coincidences like the President and fire-eater? These are just some of the questions running through our hero's mind, when suddenly—

> *SNAP* . . .
>> *ZIP* . . .
>>> *FLASH* . . .
>>>> *POP* . . .

I glanced up from ol' Betsy. My room was filling with more smoke and light than a Michael Jackson concert. Besides the now familiar special effects, there was an even more familiar face. It was hovering above my bed wearing the usual dork-oid glasses, vacuum cleaner back pack, and ever-popular toaster helmet.

"Oh, no," I sighed. "It's you again."

"No, it's not me," he said. "At least not the me you think I am. I'm a different me."

"Haven't we already had this conversation?"

"I'm not who you think I am, Wally."

"I know, I know. You're me, right."

"I'm you, but I'm not that other you."

"What other you?"

"The you you met at the ballpark."

"My head's starting to hurt again."

"Listen, that guy you met on the baseball field wasn't me. Well, it was me, but it was me from an earlier time. I'm here to tell you that when I came back to help you catch the ball I made a terrible mistake. You must go back to that game and fall down exactly like you were supposed to."

I pushed up my glasses . . . which he did exactly the same way, at exactly the same time. I tried to ignore the coincidence and asked, "Let me get this straight. You're coming back to tell me that the first you who came back was wrong and that I better listen to this you."

"That's right."

I frowned, but before I could answer there was another . . .

SNAP . . .

ZIP . . .

FLASH . . .

POP . . .

Suddenly there was another Wally hovering beside the first one. Same light, same smoke. Only now it was in stereo.

"This is too weird," I mumbled as I gave my

glasses another shove . . . just as they gave their glasses a shove. "Way too weird."

Little did I realize, the weirdness had barely begun. . . .

Chapter 3

Guest Appearances

In a matter of seconds the two Wallys were in a big-time argument. The first one was trying to convince the second that he'd made a terrible mistake, that he shouldn't have helped me catch the ball. Meanwhile, the second Wally was telling him he didn't know what he was talking about.

"I do too."

"You do not."

"Do too."

"Do not."

"Too."

"Not."

This was obviously a new definition of the phrase, *talking to yourself.* I could tell the guys were getting nowhere fast, so I raised my hands and shouted, "All right, all right!"

They both turned to me. "We're not accomplishing anything with all of this arguing," I said.

"Well, he started it."

"Did not."

"Did too."

"Not."

"Too."

"All right, all right," I repeated. "Look, can you turn off those vacuum cleaner thingies? They're pumping out more smoke than the boy's restroom over at the high school."

"Sure," they both said in unison. Then, snapping off their machines, they floated to the ground in perfect synchronization.

"Now," I said, "will one of you please tell me what's going on?"

They both answered at exactly the same time, saying exactly the same thing. "It all started back when . . ." they stopped and glared at each other.

They tried again. "Actually, it all started when—"

Once again they stopped and glared. It was incredible, like they were the same person. Come to think of it, maybe they were.

I pointed to the first one. "You start."

We all three cleared our throats, and he began. "You know how clumsy you are with mechanical stuff?"

"Of course," I said.

"Well, in about seven years you're going to try and fix your mom's vacuum cleaner."

"While at the same time making some toast and switching TV channels with your remote," the other added.

"How do you know all that?" I asked.

"Because we're you," they said in unison, "and that's what happened to us."

We all three sniffed and pushed up our glasses. I pointed to the first Wally and he continued.

"Anyway, with the vacuum cleaner, toaster, and TV remote, you will somehow get all the wires crossed and have a major accident."

"Which, of course, is the only type of accident you can have," the other Wally added.

We all sniffed and nodded.

"And, before you know it," the first Wally continued, "you will accidentally create a time machine!"

"That's right," the second Wally said. "And one of the first things I decided to do was go back in time and change our image from McDoogle the Catastrophe to McDoogle the Hero."

"But that was wrong," the first Wally insisted. "Because you changed history and made a terrible mess of the future."

"What's wrong with being a superstar?" the second Wally demanded.

"That's not how it's supposed to be," the first Wally said. He turned to me. "You know how guilty you've been feeling?"

"Well, yeah, how'd you know about that?" I asked.

"Because we're you," they said in unison.

"Oh, right."

"That guilt is because you didn't trust things to be as they should. God has a specific plan for your life and you short-circuited it."

"I didn't short circuit it," the other Wally said. "I just made it better."

"Better isn't always best."

I frowned. "You're saying I was supposed to fall in that gopher hole and make a total fool of myself."

"I'm saying you were created a certain way and there is a certain plan for your life."

The second Wally jumped in. "And I just made that plan better."

"No, you made it worse."

"Did not."

"Did too."

"Not."

"Too—"

"Guys, guys," I held up my hands again. Then turning to the first Wally I asked, "You're saying that by changing history I messed up God's plan."

"Big time."

"You can't be serious," I scoffed. "Things are going great."

"Sure, right now. But let me take you into the future to show you what will happen."

"You can do that?" I asked. "You can take me into the future?"

"Believe me, it's not anything you'll like. Not after you ruined it by catching that ball. Come with me, and let me show it to you. After that, I know you'll want to go back to the game and fix things like they should be."

"He will not," the second argued.

"He will too."

"Will not."

"Will too"

"Not."

"Too."

Suddenly everything started vibrating. Talk about rock-'n'-roll. My room shook so hard I could barely stand.

"Wha-a-a-at's hap-p-p-p-ening . . . !" I shouted.

"It-t-t-t's him!" the first Wally yelled. "He must-st-st-st have follow-ow-ow-ed me through the time warp!"

"Who-o-o-o follow-ow-ow-ed you?" I shouted back.

Before he could answer, something the size of an overfed whale started to materialize, *Star Trek* style, right there in my bed room.

"Quick-ick-ick!" the first Wally shouted to the second. "Turn on-on-on-on your Time-ime-ime Cleaner."

"Why-why-why?" the second shouted.

"He's come-ome-ome to destroy-oy-oy-oy Wally! We've got to-to-to send him-him-him back."

By now most of the whale thing was visible. But it wasn't a whale, it was a man. A humongous man. He was completely bald and about a billion years old. And he was so big that it was impossible to see his legs under the gigantic rolls of flesh. He had the saddest and angriest expression I had ever seen in my life. And he sat in what looked like the world's biggest motorized chair.

Oh, and there was one other thing: he was driving the chair directly at me. He was trying to run me over!

"Turn on-on-on your Time Cleaner!" the first Wally shouted. "Turn on your Time-ime-ime Cleaner!"

The other Wally nodded, and they both reached for their vacuum cleaner gizmos. They pulled out their hoses, snapped on their nozzle attachments, and hit their start buttons:

WOOSHHH!

More smoke and more noise.

They pointed their nozzles directly at ol' blubber boy. He looked startled, then angry. Then he began to scream:

"No . . . Don't! . . ."

"Don't listen to him!" the first Wally shouted. "Don't stop until we've sucked him back into the future!"

They moved in closer.

WOOOOSSHHHHHHH!

And to my amazement, the big guy started to break apart and be sucked into their machines.

"NOOO . . ."

And still they continued to suck him in:

"NOOOOOOOOOOOOOoooo . . ."

Until suddenly, just like that, the sumo wrestler on wheels was gone. There was nothing left. Just the usual sparks and smoke from the vacuum cleaners and toasters.

"Nice work," the first Wally shouted as he reached over and shut down his machine while the second Wally did exactly the same thing.

I wanted to say something, but it's hard to find your voice when you need CPR.

"That was just a little too close," the first Wally said. "If he had fully materialized he could have destroyed us all."

"Where did he come from?" I shuddered. "He was awful! Who was he?"

"He is the awesome and terrible WUM," the first answered.

"The what?" I asked.

"The WUM. He came from the distant future."

"What does he want?"

"His sole purpose in life is to destroy you."

"Destroy me?" I gasped. "Why?"

"Because you are the one responsible for creating his miserable existence."

"I'm responsible for creating *that?*"

"I'm afraid so."

"But how will destroying me help?"

"He knows if he kills you, he will never have existed."

"And he's that miserable?"

"Worse than you can ever imagine. That's why it's so important you come with me into the future, so I can show you everything that will happen if you refuse to correct that ball game."

"All of that over one tiny, little decision?" I asked.

"Every decision we make in our life counts,

Wally. One action leads to another and to another. Just come with me, and I'll show you. You'll meet the WUM and—"

"First of all," I argued, "there's no way I'm responsible for that . . . thing. And second, if that's who I have to face by going into the future, count me out."

"Wally—" But before he could finish, there was another:

>   *SNAP . . .*
>   *ZIP . . .*
>   *FLASH . . .*
>   *POP . . .*

"Uh-oh," I said, glancing around the room. "Now what?"

Chapter 4

Pick a Wally, Any Wally

There was more smoke and light as another Wally McDoogle, complete with the usual vacuum cleaner and toaster wardrobe, entered the room. But the grand entrances weren't over yet.

Just as soon as he finished appearing, another one started:

> *SNAP* . . .
>> *ZIP* . . .
>>> *FLASH* . . .
>>>> *POP* . . .

And then another:

> *SNAP* . . .
>> *ZIP* . . .
>>> *FLASH* . . .
>>>> *POP* . . .

And another. And, just for good measure, one last one:

SNAP . . .
ZIP . . .
FLASH . . .
POP . . .

By the time I was done dropping by to visit myself, there were six Wally McDoogles from the future.

Incredible. Six Wallys plus me. That made seven Wally McDoogles all in the same room. All doing the same thing at the same time. All pushing up our glasses at the same time, all saying the same thing at the same time. I could only shake my head in wonder and pray that one of us didn't suddenly have to go to the bathroom. Then things could have gotten really crowded.

"What are you all doing here?" I shouted over their roaring vacuum cleaners.

"You've got to go into the future," they cried desperately. "You've got to see what you've done!"

Before I could answer there was a sudden knocking on my door. "Wally?"

I froze. It was Mom.

"Wally, what's going on in there? Have you got the vacuum cleaner going?"

Before I could catch myself, all seven of us answered, "Yes."

"How sweet," she said. "But there's no need to vacuum, honey. I'll do that this afternoon. Right now you need to get dressed. You don't want to be late for school."

I spun around to my radio clock. After brushing off the usual assortment of dirty socks and underwear, I finally saw the time—7:15. My, my how time flies when you're having a major nightmare.

Unfortunately, this was no nightmare. . . .

"Wally, do you hear me?"

"Yes, Mom," all seven of us answered in unison.

"And there's no need to shout," she said. "I can hear perfectly well."

As she walked away we all let out a sigh of relief. "That was close," I said. "Mom's got a strong heart, but seeing six older versions of me crowded in this room would be enough to send anybody to Intensive Care."

"She wouldn't see older versions of you," the six other me's said in unison.

"She wouldn't?"

"No. Since she doesn't know you to be any older than you are now, this is how old she'd see us."

"You mean everybody who sees you guys will think they see me?"

"Exactly."

"Hmmm," I said. "This could prove interesting."

* * * * *

Unfortunately, it wasn't so interesting when all six of them insisted on following me downstairs. It wasn't too bad until we all tripped over Collision the cat (who did not get her name by accident), and we all tumbled down the steps exactly the same way.

But crashing down the stairs in a tangled knot of twenty-eight arms and legs wasn't the main problem. The main problem was Dad's reaction to all that tumbling and crashing.

"It's an earthquake!" he yelled, running through the house grabbing flashlights and portable radios. "Everyone crawl under the table! It's an earthquake; it's an earthquake!" (Growing up in California made Dad kinda paranoid in the earthquake department. The fact that we haven't had one in this area since about 254 B.C. makes no difference. "It just means we're way overdue," he keeps insisting.)

Knowing Dad's heart was no stronger than Mom's, my six futuristic clones managed to hide before he saw them. Unfortunately, they all thought of the same hiding place and crammed themselves into the same tiny broom closet. Even that was okay until one of them started sneezing . . . which, of course, meant all of them sneezing . . . in perfect unison. Poor Dad, not only did he think we were having an earthquake, but now he was sure our house was under attack.

But that wasn't as bad as our trip to school. . . .

"Come on, guys," I said. "At least let me go to school by myself."

"Not until you agree to go into the future with us," they said. "Besides, if the WUM should return, you'll need us to protect you and suck him back into the future again."

"I still can't believe I'm responsible for that thing," I said.

"Believe it," they answered.

Of course, I wanted to ask a million more questions, but I also wanted to get rid of them. I mean, let's face it, it's dangerous enough to have one of me around. Can you imagine having six more? I just wasn't sure if our little town could handle it. To be honest, I wasn't sure if our little planet could.

Still, there was no way I was going into the future with these guys, especially if it meant meeting that Overeater's Anonymous reject with the bad attitude.

Although my clones refused to leave, I did

convince them to make a few changes so they
wouldn't draw quite so much attention to themselves.

First, they left their vacuum cleaners and toasters in my room (which made the place look like
an appliance sale at Sears). Next, they changed
into some of my clothes. And, though they still
insisted on going to school with me, they did agree
it would be better to take separate routes so no
one would see us together.

It was a great idea. Except the part where I
wasn't paying attention and stepped out in front
of Mr. Pipplepucker's Pontiac. The poor guy had
to swerve onto the sidewalk, taking out a fire
hydrant which began spraying more water than
Old Faithful.

But it didn't stop there. . . .

It seems Middletown had a rash of identical
accidents at exactly the same time. In fact, when
we were done, the entire city was covered in
about three feet of water. . . . And there were
no unsmashed Pontiacs to be found.

Luckily, school was a lot better. For starters,
there were seven of us and only seven periods.
Now I'm no math whiz, but I figured if we traded
off, each of us would only have to sit through
one class apiece.

Not a bad deal.

An even better deal was P.E. Our regular teacher, Coach Killroy, was out for the week. That left his assistant, an ex-Marine sergeant by the name of Gus Gravelchewer. Ol' Gus had one goal and one goal only: to make sure that every day every student suffered complete physical and emotional exhaustion.

Today, he thought it would be especially fun having us run around the track a gazillion times. Since I usually finish such workouts on my hands and knees, wheezing my lungs out, you can imagine Gravelchewer's surprise to see me cross the finish line first . . . and without even breaking a sweat. (The fact that there were plenty of bleachers and concession stands for the other six Wallys to race out from behind and take over, did a lot to explain my sudden physical fitness.)

But it didn't explain Billy Buckleman's behavior. As a star athlete, he was always great in P.E. But not today. Today he barely finished the race.

As we trudged toward the showers I pulled up along side him and asked, "Hey, Billy, you okay?"

"Oh, hi, Wally." I don't want to say the guy sounded down, but if his voice were any flatter it would be in the House of Pancakes.

"What's wrong?" I asked.

"I didn't sleep much last night. I just kept thinking about how I almost messed up yesterday's big

game. I couldn't believe how I fell down like that.
I'm sure glad you were there to save us."

"Hey," I said, trying to fight back my returning
guilt, "it was just one of those things."

"I don't think so, Wally. I tell you, I just don't
know if I have what it takes to be an athlete any-
more."

I came to a stop and watched as he headed into
the building. Billy Buckleman was great. Everyone
figured someday he'd be a professional ball player
or an Olympic athlete or both. But now . . .

"See what I mean?"

I spun around and saw all six Wallys behind
me.

"And that's only the beginning," they said.

"Are you telling me, by catching that ball I also
changed Billy's future?"

"That's right," they said.

I turned to the first Wally, the one who had
helped me catch the ball. "Is that true?" I asked.

"Well, yeah," he mumbled, staring at the ground,
"but it seemed like a small price to pay to make
Wally McDoogle a hero that everybody loves."

I was feeling worse than ever.

"Wally," the others insisted, "you've got to come
with us. You've got to let us show you—"

But that was as far as they got. Suddenly the
ground started shaking again.

"Oh, no-o-o-o!" they shouted.

"Wha-wha-what's happening-ing-ing?" I cried.

"It's the WUM. Run, Wally, ru-un-un!"

Now, I normally would have stuck around to see what was happening. But since my ditto buddies had left their Time Cleaners in my room, and since I'm strongly allergic to dying, I figured now was as good a time as any to make like a cheap pair of pants and split. The last thing in the world I wanted to see was this Free Willy wannabe. Especially if he was trying to destroy me.

I spun around and began running for all I was worth, which if I didn't hurry, would be two cents less than nothing.

Chapter 5

Decisions, Decisions

By the time I got home, six more of me were standing guard outside my house. They all had their vacuum cleaner thingies strapped to their backs with the hoses and nozzle attachments aimed and ready.

"Hey, how'd you fellows beat me here?" I shouted as I headed up the walk.

"We didn't," they said in unison. "We're not the same you's you left behind at school. We're new you's."

"You mean," I swallowed hard, feeling another headache coming on, "you're a whole other group of me's from the future?"

"That's right!" they all said.

"So that makes twelve of you now?" I asked.

"Thirteen counting yourself," they said.

"Oh yeah. But why are you here?"

"We've come to warn you that your time is almost up. If you don't hurry and come with us into the future, we'll be destroyed by the WUM."

"You mean *I'll* be destroyed."

"If you're a goner, we're all goners," they said.

I nodded. They had a point. There was no getting around it. It was time to face the facts and be brave. Time to buckle down and suck it up. Time to throw myself down on the ground and have a good cry.

"How long before this WUM thing shows up?" I asked.

They looked at their watches. "In exactly nine minutes and forty-five seconds."

"Can you give me a couple of minutes to make up my mind?"

"Certainly," they said as they glanced at their watches again. "As long as it doesn't take over nine minutes and thirty-eight seconds. Make that nine minutes and thirty-five seconds. Er, nine minutes and—"

"Yeah, yeah," I said. "I get the idea."

I had to make a decision, and I had to make it fast. I raced up to my room, tore into another Gooey Chewy bar, and began pacing. What should I do? Go into the future and face the 10,000-pound monster completely unarmed? Or stay behind and face the 10,000-pound monster completely unarmed?

Decisions, decisions.

Then I spotted her. Ol' Betsy. Writing stories had always helped me make decisions before. Why should this time be any different?

I walked across the room, turned her on, and continued my superhero story:

When we last left Flame Boy he was flying toward the obviously offensive and astonishingly awful glob of Sunscreen #85 that the arch-anarchist Arctic Guy (say that seven times fast) had placed between the sun and Earth.

Back on the ground it is getting so cold that the people not only see their breath, but they can actually pluck it out of the air, take it home, and thaw it out in the oven if they ever get short of it.

Higher and higher our hero soars. First through the stratosphere, then the ionosphere, and then, just when he's about to run out of spheres, he spots a giant floating refrigerator.

Being a highly intelligent superhero, he suspects this is no ordinary refrigerator, so he quickly adjusts his course

to investigate. He arrives at the door
and with a mighty tug (and secret hopes
that there is still some fried chicken
left over from the night before), he
pulls it open to see:

"Arctic Guy!" he gasps.

A frost-covered midget in a ski mask
and bow tie looks up. He is busy eating a frozen TV dinner (what did you
expect) sprinkled with a healthy por-
tion of Fudgesicle shavings. "Do I know
you?" he sneers.

His breath is so cold that it immediately turns Flame Boy's fire an icy
blue. Our hero tries to answer but
begins shivering so hard he can barely
speak.

No one's sure what made Arctic Guy so
cold. Some say it was teenage rebellion
against his mother. Seems she left
him in the car one too many summer days
with the windows rolled up and the heat
turned on high. Even that wouldn't have
been so bad if it weren't for the three
layers of long underwear she made him
wear. (Being the overprotective type,
his mom was always afraid her little
darling would catch a chill.)

Others believe it came from watching one too many *Frosty the Snowman* reruns during Christmas time. Hey, everybody needs a role model.

Finally, there's the ever-popular theory that he was eating so many snow cones that his dad said he'd eventually turn into one. And always wanting to keep his dad happy, he did his best to obey.

Whatever the reason, Arctic Guy is definitely giving our hero a chilly reception. Talk about a cold shoulder. The kid is really starting to freeze up.

But knowing he's a superhero, and that superheroes can't lose (at least not this early in the story), Flame Boy reaches down into his very coals and burns with all of his might. Soon, he creates enough heat to thaw his super-hero mouth. And with a loud and commanding voice, he bellows:

"Hi there."

Arctic Guy gives him an icy look. "Who, or should I say, *what* are you?"

"My name is Flame Boy, and I've come to fight for truth, justice, and the American weight."

"That's *way*, stupid. 'Truth, Justice, and the American Way'."

"Oh, thanks," Flame Boy says. "I'm kinda new at this."

"What's the matter? Couldn't they afford to send a real superhero?"

Before our hero realizes he's been insulted, Arctic Guy leans back and blows a mighty blast of super-cold air. It is so chilly that Flame Boy's flame immediately begins to flicker.

But that's nothing compared to Arctic Guy's breath. It's not that it's bad, but it would sure be better if the guy cut back on those onion-flavored frozen yogurts. Even that wouldn't be so bad if he'd just stop with the garlic and clam sauce toppings.

But the freezing cold and foul smell are nothing compared to the overwhelming force of the wind. It's a hurricane. So strong that it is all Flame Boy can do to hang on to the side of the refrigerator and keep from being blown off. But as he hangs on his flame starts to flicker out.

And still Arctic Guy blows.

Oh no. What a terrible dilemma. If Flame Boy lets go, he'll tumble back

to Earth where the chances of finding
another fire-eater to shoot him back
into the sky are pretty slim even for
this story.

Yet, if he hangs on to the side of
the refrigerator his very flame will
be blown out (if he doesn't die first
from the smell of onion, garlic, and
clam sauce).

Then, just when his indecision couldn't
be getting any more indecisive—

Suddenly I stopped typing. I had my answer.
Like Flame Boy, I had to do something. I had to
make up my mind. I couldn't just sit around and
wait to be destroyed.

I saved the Flame Boy story, shut down ol' Betsy,
and walked over to my second story window to
look outside. It was a scary sight. Six Wally
McDoogles all standing guard with toaster helmets and vacuum cleaners.

Off in the distance, something caught my eye.
It was then I realized the nightmare had only
begun. . . .

Less than a block away, running toward me as
fast as their little tootsies could carry them, were
the other six me's.

And directly behind them, closing in fast on his

giant electric-powered chair, was the dreaded WUM.

There was no time to waste. I reached down to pull up the window, but it was stuck. I tried harder. Still nothing. It was then my razor-sharp intellect kicked into gear, and I remembered it would be easier to open the window if you unlocked it. I tell you, sometimes having such intelligence can really be scary.

I threw open the window and leaned out to shout, "Okay, guys, I'm ready. Let's go."

The six Wallys standing guard with their time machines looked up to me. "Are you sure?" they asked.

"Of course I'm not sure. But when has that stopped us from doing anything in the past?"

"Or the future," they agreed.

I headed back to scoop up ol' Betsy and returned to the window. Without a word, the six guard Wallys aimed their vacuum cleaner nozzles directly up at me. In perfect unison they snapped on their machines and:

WOOOOOOSSSSSSSHHHHHHHhhhhhh . . .

Chapter 6
Grand Central

I don't want to say time travel is uncomfortable, but picture a hungry boy and a very delicious hamburger. Now picture that hungry boy gobbling down that very delicious hamburger.

How is that so uncomfortable, you say? Just ask the hamburger.

First everything went black. Then I was pitched to and fro. Then fro and to. I was toasted. I was baked. I was sliced, diced, and turned into julienne fries. And, just when I thought I was done with all the food comparisons, I was fried, poached, and scrambled.

I'm not sure how long I was traveling like that. (It's hard to keep track of time when your body is being pulverized into pre-chewed food goo.) All I know is I eventually landed, face first, in some very soft grass. My heart swelled with gratitude. Not because the traveling was over and not because I landed face first. I was simply grateful for still having a face.

I opened my eyes and sat up. I was in an incredible rain forest. Giant trees, lush ferns, and trickling waterfalls surrounded me on all sides.

"Wow!" I cried as I rose to my feet. (Not because of the beauty, but because I still had feet.) I made a quick check of the rest of my body parts. Talk about lucky. I only had a minimum number of bruised body parts and broken legs.

And luckier still, there were absolutely no other Wallys floating around. Not a single vacuum cleaner whooshing, not a single toaster burning. Everything was incredibly quiet and very, very peaceful.

I tell you, if this was the future, you could sign me up for it any day. Of course, there seemed to be a noticeable lack of shopping malls, movie theaters, and video games, but I was sure I could find some way of wasting all my time and money.

I noticed a nearby stream winding through the ferns. I picked up ol' Betsy and made my way toward the water. The bank of the stream was soft and mossy. A large gray rock rested nearby, and I started to climb it. It was a lot softer than the rocks back home. But that wasn't the only difference. It also felt a little warmer. Then, of course, there were the eyes, nose, and teeth.

EYES, NOSE, AND TEETH?

Whatever it was I was climbing, suddenly stirred awake. And before I could hop off, it rose into the air.

How odd, I thought. *Not only is this rock alive, but it can fly.*

Next I noticed that this particular living rock just happened to be attached to a very large living neck.

How odd, a living rock attached to a very large living neck.

Which was attached to an even larger living body.

How odd, a living rock attached to a living neck which was attached to a—"Great Jurassic Park!" I shouted. "I'm on a dinosaur!"

Now, I'm sure all you dinosaur freaks out there want to know exactly what type of dinosaur I was on. And having one of those inquiring minds, I normally would have found out. But, at that particular moment, I was somewhat preoccupied with another tiny little matter like . . .

RUNNING FOR MY LIFE!

I leaped off Dino Boy and hit the ground just in time to do my usual tumbling and rolling routine:

Ouch! Ooch! Ow! Boy does that smart!

Then I jumped up and dashed into the forest as fast as I could.

Unfortunately my new friend had the same idea (without the tumbling and rolling part). Apparently he didn't appreciate being awakened from his beauty sleep (and with his looks I could see why), so he lumbered to his feet and started to chase after me.

THUMP, THUMP, THUMP. . .

The ground shook with every step.

Now, I've never been very good at dinosaur tag (especially the part where they tag you "it" and smash your little body three feet into the ground). So I did what I always do when I'm in trouble. I screamed my head off:

"SOMEBODY HELP ME!"

But there was nobody there to answer. Well, nobody except this outdated reptile with the bad disposition. And by the way he was snapping and snarling, I figured the type of help he had in mind was not exactly the type I needed.

Directly ahead of me I saw a large field that looked like somebody had cleared it. I knew I had to stay in the forest and use the trees for cover, so

I veered to the right, all the time doing what I do best—screaming:

"HELP ME! HELP ME! HELP ME! . . ."

Meanwhile, the pet reject from the Flintstones was right behind me doing what he did best:

THUMP, THUMP, THUMP . . .

His feet were coming closer and closer.

Now, not being entirely sure what I wanted to be when I grew up, but knowing it wasn't dinosaur toe jam, I found the strength to run even harder. What was going on? What was this Barney wannabe doing in my future? Come to think of it, what was I about to become in his present?

And then I heard it:

"Wally, over here!"

I looked over to the clearing and saw all twelve of my little photocopy-me buddies floating above it. "We cleared this field for you," they shouted. "Come on!"

"What's going on?" I cried.

"We made a mistake. Instead of transporting you to the future, we accidentally sent you into the past."

Of course. Why didn't I think of that? Now everything made sense. The rain forest, the dinosaur, the fact that twelve of me had tried to do something right. No wonder it turned out so wrong. This wasn't just a normal kind of McDoogle catastrophe. This was a McDoogle catastrophe times twelve!

"What do I do?" I shouted.

"Run out into the middle of this clearing."

"What?"

"Our Time Cleaners are all set. Run into the middle of the clearing, and we'll suck you into the future."

"If I run out there, Dino boy will see me and kill me."

"Not if we zap you first."

"Are you crazy?"

"No, just a little clumsy and accident prone. Hurry!" they shouted. "He's almost on top of you!"

I looked over my shoulder and saw his giant feet pounding right behind me.

THUMP, THUMP, THUMP . . .

The way I figured it, I had two choices:

1. Continue starring in this prehistoric movie gone haywire, or . . .
2. Make a break for it and hope the boys with the household appliances would get it right.

It was a tough decision. Fortunately, old Big Foot was there to give me a hand. Well, actually a tooth . . . actually several teeth.

His head appeared behind me, and before I could get out of the way, he opened his mighty jaws and clamped down. Luckily, all he managed to grab was the belt loop to my jeans.

But that was enough.

He lifted me high into the air.

"AUGHHHHhhhh . . ."

Next he began tossing me back and forth like a rag doll.

That was the bad news. The good news was that Mom always made me wear my brother's hand-me-downs, which were always about three sizes too big. This came in handy when I wanted to look like a bag lady or some hip-hopper. It came in even handier when being picked up by a cranky dinosaur.

The pants were so big that it only took three shakes of Dino's head before I slipped out of them. And, as luck would have it, my Fruit of the Looms and I flew right into the open field. Right where the twelve of me were standing and aiming their vacuum cleaner nozzles.

"Ready!" they shouted.

"Please, God," I prayed.

"Aim!"

"Please, please."

"Fire!"

"Please, please, please—"

WOOOOOOSSSSSSSHHHHHHHhhhhhh . . .

* * * * *

Once again I was sailing through darkness, feeling a lot like a pre-chewed Big Mac.

When I finally landed, it was on something far less pleasant than the soft grass of the rain forest. In fact, it felt a lot like a bunch of computer monitors, keyboards, and hot coffee.

SIZZLE. POP. SPARK. SPARK. SHORT. SHORT.

Come to think of it, it sounded like a bunch of computer monitors and keyboards . . . with the hot coffee spilling all over them:

SIZZLE. POP. SPARK. SPARK.
SHORT. SHORT. SHORT. SHORT. SHORT.

I opened my eyes. Yup, just as I expected. There I was sprawled out on a bunch of broken monitors and sparking computer terminals . . . with spilled cups of coffee pouring everywhere.

"We have touchdown!" somebody shouted. "Mr. McDoogle is in the lab."

There was a spattering of applause as I sat up and looked around.

The place was like a giant control room. It was perfectly round with a dozen people sitting around an oval table with computer monitors in front of them. They were all dressed in futuristic clothing that looked like part cellophane wrap and part aluminum foil. Oh, and one other thing . . .

They were all me.

I gave kind of a half wave. "Hi, guys," I said.

"Hi," they all said in perfect unison. "Welcome to the future, Wally."

I looked up to see another one of myselves holding out his hand and offering to help me off all of the smashed computer stuff.

"Thanks," I said, throwing my feet over the side and noticing I was wearing the same getup as the rest of them. "Sorry about ruining all the equipment."

"We were expecting it," he grinned. "After all, we're all Wally McDoogles, right?"

"Yeah, uh right," I said, suddenly unthrilled about the idea. "So exactly where am I this time?"

"This time you're where you're supposed to be," he said. "Twenty five years into the future. In fact, we built this little room just for your visit."

"No kidding?" I looked around. It was pretty impressive. Besides the dozen me's sitting in front of their computer screens, there was a giant 3-D

TV image floating in the center. A giant 3-D TV image of a very familiar looking person running to catch a very familiar looking baseball at the All-City Championship baseball game.

"Hey," I said, "that's me."

"And me," the other twelve said in unison, "before we tried to change things."

"Oh, that again," I said, pushing up my glasses at exactly the same time they did.

"Yes, that again," the first Wally said sadly.

"Listen, how can changing one little thing cause so much trouble?"

He sighed and answered. "There was a plan, Wally, and we messed it up. And by messing it up everything went haywire." He reached for a piece of paper on the nearby console. (It took a little doing to find one that wasn't soaked in coffee.) Once he found it, he drew a straight line across it. Next he wrote a few numbers along the top. "This line, here," he said. "Let's pretend it's God's will for your life. And these numbers here are your age."

0 ├──────────────50──────────────┤ 100

"Way back here at age thirteen you decided you wanted to make one little change." He added a

tiny line that angled down ever so slightly from
the first.

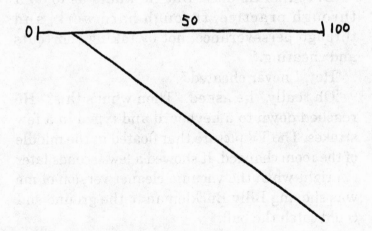

"You can barely see it," I said. "That's not enough
to do anything."

"Not at first. But what happens if you keep following that line out to say five years from now, or
ten, or thirty, or fifty, or a hundred years?" He continued drawing the new angle until it ran off the
bottom of the page.

"See how that one little difference gets bigger
and bigger as the years go on?"

I nodded.

"That's how it is with God's will. It may not seem like a lot at first, but if we keep following our way instead of His, and if we don't turn around and ask Him to fix it, things get worse and worse and worse."

I stared at the line. "And that's what you think I've done?" I said. "Made a little change at the beginning that keeps getting worse and worse just like that line?"

He nodded.

"But what's wrong with catching a ball? Doesn't God expect us to do our best?"

"Of course He does. But He wants us to do it through practice, through hard work, and through perseverance, not by taking shortcuts and cheating."

"Hey, I never cheated."

"Oh really," he asked. "Then what's this?" He reached down to a keyboard and typed in a few strokes. The TV picture that floated in the middle of the room changed. It showed a few seconds later . . . right when the vacuum cleaner version of me was shoving Billy Buckleman to the ground so I could catch the ball.

"Okay," I admitted, "maybe that wasn't so nice. But you can't tell me that a bunch of other stuff happened just because of that one little detail."

"Everything on that diagonal time line happened

because you and I tried to rewrite history, because you and I tried to out-think God."

Unfortunately, he was starting to make sense. So I did exactly what I do when Mom and Dad make too much sense . . . I changed subjects.

"So where are all your Time Cleaner thingies?" I asked, as I looked around the room. "What happened to all those vacuum cleaners and toasters that are supposed to send me into the future?"

"Oh, we still have them. But we thought it would be safer if you just watched the future up on that giant video projection."

I looked up to the TV image floating in the middle of the room. "That can show the future, too?" I asked.

"Yes. We've got every year of your life recorded, from the moment you first caught that ball, until the moment you die."

"You're kidding."

"This is no joke, Wally . . . except for all the funny stuff that keeps happening to you for the rest of your life."

I gave a weak smile. "How much can I see?" I asked.

"We figured three sections would be enough. Three very different times in your future that will help you understand why you must go back and fix things."

"And if I don't?"

He turned to one of the nearby Wallys and ordered, "Put up the first Wally scene."

"Yes, sir," the other Wally replied as he typed something on his keyboard. "Wally McDoogle ten years into the future."

Immediately, the first picture of me was replaced by another. I was older, wearing sun glasses and real cool clothes made of gold thread. And, as always, I was munching away on another Gooey Chewy bar.

Oh, and one other thing . . . I was being mobbed by a thousand fans.

I raised my eyebrows. "That doesn't look so bad," I said.

But before anyone could answer, a blaring alarm sounded.

"What's that?" I cried.

The first version of me shouted to another me across the room. "Security, report!"

"We have a breach at the main entrance," the other me shouted back.

"Is it him?"

"Yes, sir. WUM has come back from the year 2109. He is in the adjoining hall and should be breaking through that wall behind us right about—"

Suddenly the wall behind us exploded.

"—NOW!"

The nightmarish creature plowed into the room.

He was uglier than I remembered and looked like he'd put on a couple extra tons.

The others in the room leaped to their feet in panic. But there was no need for them to worry. The WUM wasn't after them. He quickly scanned the room and spotted his real target.

Me.

"Hi there," I kinda squeaked.

He returned the greeting with an agonizing wail, aimed his giant motorized chair directly at me, and started forward.

I grabbed ol' Betsy, dove over the table, and made a beeline for the nearest exit. Unfortunately, that beeline took me directly through the TV picture floating in the air.

"No, Wally, not that way!" the twelve Wallys shouted.

But they were too late. I had to get out of there, and if it meant running through a floating TV picture, so what. After all, it was only air, right?

Well, not quite.

As I leaped through the picture, expecting to come out the other side, I discovered a curious fact. I hadn't leaped *through* the picture. I had leaped *into* the picture.

I had entered the future exactly ten years from when I had first caught the baseball.

Chapter 7

All Dressed Up and Everywhere to Go

There was more screaming and shouting than when someone accidently changes channels during the Super Bowl. More shoving and pushing than an after-Christmas sale at the Mall. Everyone was gathered around me yelling and pulling and crying and screaming, "We love you Wally. . . . Please, let me have your autograph. . . . Oh, Mr. McDoogle, you are soooo cool. . . ."

I searched the crowd trying to find where the futuristic version of myself had gone. But it was impossible to make out anything through the endless sea of faces and arms. An endless sea of faces and arms all looking and reaching out to . . .

Hey, wait a minute. Why are they all looking at *me?*

"Just sign here, Mr. McDoogle. . . . Just kiss my baby, Mr. McDoogle."

Once again my keen intellect went into overtime and once again I came to a genius conclusion:

Something wasn't right.

Where had the other Wally McDoogle gone—the one with the Gooey Chewy bar and all the cool gold clothes that I saw up on the screen? It was then I glanced down and noticed that I just happened to be the one holding a Gooey Chewy bar and wearing all the cool clothes.

Uh-oh . . .

Somehow, I had become that other Wally . . .

Another group of crowd members reached out to me. But instead of offering me their books to autograph or their babies to kiss, this group was more interested in taking. Not a lot, just a little something to remember the moment by. . . .

"Mr. McDoogle, can I have this lock of your hair?"

"OW!"

"Mr. McDoogle, you won't be missing this coat."

"Hey that's my—"

"Just a little piece of your shirt."

RRIIIP

"Let me have a piece, too."

Rriiip . . . Rriiip . . .

"Hey, are these pants real gold?"

Rip, rip, tear, tear . . .
Shiver . . . shiver . . .

The sound of ripping and tearing came from what was left of my clothes.

The shivering came from what was left of me.

Suddenly things were getting awfully chilly. Fortunately, I still had on my underwear, so at least I was—

"Hey, look everybody, gold Fruit of the Looms!"

And then, just when things couldn't possibly get any colder (or more embarrassing) I heard an old, familiar voice:

"All right everybody, stand back! Step aside!"

Through the crowd I saw my old buddy, Wall Street! She was older, but there was no mistaking her face or the look of greed in her eyes. She pushed her way through the mob with the help of a couple of bodyguards the size of the Dallas Cowboys offensive line.

"Wall Street!" I shouted.

"Hang on, Wally, we'll be right there!" She continued pushing and shoving. "Get out of the way, step aside!"

For the most part, they obeyed her. The ones who didn't suddenly found themselves turning into forward passes or punted field goals, courtesy of the two bodyguards.

When she arrived she threw a blanket around me. Then the big guys lifted me up and carried me to a limousine just slightly smaller than the state of Rhode Island. I don't want to say it was too big or fancy, but I thought the outdoor swimming pool and tennis court in the back were just a bit much.

The big boys opened the door, and as the crowd surged forward, they threw me inside.

"Wow," I cried, "that was unbelievable!"

Wall Street tumbled in after me. "It happens every time," she grumbled.

"What's that?" I asked as the limo began pulling away.

"If I've told you once, I've told you a hundred times," she said as she produced her calculator and began punching keys, "when you go out in public, you've got to wear a disguise."

"I do?"

"Somebody as rich and famous as you should never be out in public alone. Otherwise this sort of thing is bound to happen."

"It is?"

She continued her figuring without looking up. "Fortunately, our losses are not as severe as the last time. The gold coat, shirt, pants, and underwear only cost $2,752.24. Subtract that from your total net worth of $34 million, and you're still worth $33,997,247.76."

"That's how much money I've got?"

"Minus, of course, seventy-five thousand dollars to me for rescuing you."

"Seventy-five thousand dollars!"

"Of course," she said. "That's always been my fee."

"Of course," I said, pretending to know what I was talking about.

"Unless you want to throw in an extra ten-thousand-dollar bonus."

"Why's that?"

"It looks like I might have chipped a nail."

I smiled and shook my head in quiet amazement. What a comfort to know that some things never change. Apparently Wall Street was finally getting around to making all that money she wanted. And by the looks of things, she was making it all off of me.

I looked out the window. I didn't know how I'd gotten so rich and famous, but, I tell you, if this is what the future held, it was okay by me.

"Here," she said, shoving a contract under my nose, "sign this."

"What is it?"

"Your agreement to endorse Gooey Chewy bars on your next TV special. In return they'll supply you with three cases of Gooey Chewys a week."

"Cool," I said as I grabbed her pen and scrawled my signature on the paper.

Meanwhile, Wall Street had pressed the intercom button to signal the driver. The man answered through the speaker. "Yes, Ms. *crunch-crunch-crunch* Street?"

I recognized him instantly. (The fact that his mouth was crammed with a thousand potato chips made it a little easier.) "Opera," I cried, "is that you?"

"Yes, Mr. *munch-munch-munch* McDoogle. I am quite relieved that you *crunch-munch-smack* did not sustain any major injury during that recent altercation. Perhaps—"

"Opera," I interrupted, "why are you being so polite? It's me, Wally."

"Yes, it certainly is, Mr. McDoogle."

"A fellow dork-oid, remember?"

"Anything you *burp* say, Mr. McDoogle."

"What's wrong with—"

Before I could finish, Wall Street clicked off the button and scowled at me. "I've told you before, you must stop being so friendly with the servants."

"Servants?"

"As your business manager, I must remind you of your position when dealing with commoners."

"*Commoners?*"

She nodded and pressed the intercom again. "How soon before we arrive at the stadium?"

"Ten or fifteen minutes," Opera answered.

"Which is it?" she demanded. "Ten or fifteen? We have a tight schedule to follow."

"Sorry, Ms. Street. Our estimated time of arrival is twelve minutes and twenty-seven seconds."

"That's better."

She released the button and without looking at me said, "Once you get there you will have four and a half minutes to change into your tuxedo. Of course the President will want to meet with you before you go on stage, but you'll only be able to give him a few seconds."

"The President?" I croaked. "Of what?"

"Very funny," she said. "Oh, and this time try not to spill your hot chocolate all over the First Lady. And if you do, let the Secret Service dab it up. Last time it took six weeks for her broken ribs to heal."

"Okay . . ."

Wall Street cocked her head sideways, as if listening, and then rolled down her window. We could hear people shouting. Thousands of them. They were all chanting one word over and over again. One word I was very familiar with:

"Wall-ly, Wall-ly, Wall-ly, Wall-ly"

"Is that . . . me?" I asked.

"Of course it's you," Wall Street laughed. "All 90,000 fans in that stadium are calling out your name. They've all put down big bucks to see the great Wally McDoogle perform."

"Perform?" I felt a wave of panic. "What am I supposed to do?"

"Why, just be you. Of course you'll want to fall down a few dozen times so they get their money's worth."

"Falling down?" I asked. "That's good?"

"Of course it's good. That's why they buy all your instructional videotapes, so they can learn to be just as clumsy and klutzy as you are. Look over there."

I looked out the window and saw dozens of people along the road all throwing themselves down on the ground or walking into things.

"You're the hit of the decade, Wally. Everybody wants to be like you."

"But . . . why . . . how?"

"You know how," she scoffed. "It started way back when you caught that ball at the All-City Championship. From there your team went to the Nationals where, of course, you were your usual clumsy and dork-oid self."

"Of course," I said.

"That's when the TV producer saw you and hired you to star in your own TV series where you just did what you normally do."

"Stumble around and make a total fool of myself?"

"Exactly. And suddenly you became an overnight success. Now everybody wants to be like you."

I sat back in the seat absolutely amazed. I couldn't believe it. . . . I was loved by thousands of fans, had millions of dollars, starred in my own TV series, and had an unlimited supply of Gooey Chewys. What could be better?

I turned back to Wall Street, but she was hunched over her calculator and obviously didn't want to be bothered. Since we still had a few more minutes before we arrived at the stadium, I reached down to get ol' Betsy. Now seemed like a good time to work on my superhero story. Not that what was happening to Flame Boy could be any weirder than what was happening to me. But some habits are hard to break. . . .

Chapter 8
A Not-So-Bright Future

When we last left Flame Boy he was having a hard time getting a grip. Not only on trying to be a superhero, but also on the refrigerator door that he was clinging to. The more Arctic Guy blasts him with his Arctic breath, the more Flame Boy realizes that he'll have to brush up on his skydiving.

No problem...except that he's never skydived in his life.

Even that's no biggie...except for the part of not having a parachute. And, since he hates making bad impressions (especially when it's his soft little body in that big hard ground), well, you can see why he might be a little nervous.

But Arctic Guy continues to blow and blow as our hero continues to slip and slip until he finally loses his grip and falls.

"AUGHHhhhh..."

But, as luck would have it (along with some very clever writing on this author's part), Flame Boy suddenly remembers his training at the University of Superherohood.

Quicker than you can say, "I figured something like this would happen," Flame Boy grabs his legs and curls into a tight little fireball.

A neat trick, but his version of the cannonball dive only makes him fall faster. So he tries his jack-knife, then his one-and-a-half gainer. All very impressive and good enough to make the Olympic diving team. But unless they hold the competition in the next 23.4 seconds, it is doubtful he'll be picking up any medals. And if he doesn't hurry with a solution, he'll be the one they're picking up.

Then, in a flash of inspiration (what other type of inspiration can someone made of fire have?) our hero remembers.

He may not have all the cool superhero
gizmos and gadgets of the other superheroes, but he does have one unique
ability . . . he can do the entire
"Battle Hymn of the Republic" with
burps.

"So what good will that do him?" you
ask.

None. But he thought you should know.

Wait a minute! He suddenly remembers
he has *two* unique abilities. Granted,
the burping is great for getting sent
away from the table (especially when
cooked broccoli is on the menu). But his
second ability is even better. . . .
He's made out of fire! (Good thing he
doesn't think it's his quick thinking.)

Quickly he spreads out his arms. The
wind catches his flames and begins to
fan them. Brighter and brighter he
glows, bigger and bigger he grows.

Soon he is covering the entire sky.

What luck! Not only is he saving his
life, but also by spreading his flames
across the sky, he immediately begins
heating up the earth. Suddenly there is
more warmth than a *Little House on
the Prairie* rerun. More hot air than

a political debate. Arctic Guy's plot has been foiled. Who needs the sun now? Who needs to worry about the giant glob of Sunscreen #85 blocking its rays?

The day is saved.

Well, almost.

It seems there are a couple of kinks still to be ironed out. First, there are all those Californians complaining about their fading tans. Things may have warmed up, but you can't get a tan from regular fire. (See how educational these stories can be.)

Second, there is the President. Not only is he still a little cranky about not getting his pizza, but he also remembers it's an election year and he must impress everyone to get their votes.

So, even though Flame Boy has saved the day, the President suddenly launches 734 nuclear missiles to *out* save Flame Boy's save. All 734 nuclear missiles are heading straight toward the giant blob of Sunscreen #85.

Everybody is impressed. And, except for the fact that the explosion will poison the atmosphere and kill everyone on Earth, the President can rest assured that he now has everyone's vote.

Things couldn't be better...except that while he is destroying all life as we know it, he'll also be destroying all those *Brady Bunch* reruns that he wanted to save. (If you think he's cranky now, just wait until he can no longer hear those old favorite strains about, "...a lovely lady who is bringing up three very lovely girls....")

Oh no, what will happen now that he's fired those missiles?

How will Earth survive?

More importantly, will our beloved President ever get those deluxe anchovy pizzas with extra cheese?

All these questions and more are running through our hero's head, when suddenly—

SNAP ...
ZIP ...
FLASH ...
POP ...

I looked up from ol' Betsy. Once again everything had dropped into super-slow motion—

Wall Street calculating my money, the fans in the stadium chanting my name, even the speed of our limo (which was now moving slower than a kid on his way to summer school).

Oh, and I saw one other thing. Actually twelve of them.

Yes sir, there were my old buddies, all hovering around the car, all wearing their standard issue vacuum cleaner backpacks and toaster helmets.

I rolled down the window. "Hi, guys."

"Hi," they said as we all pushed up our glasses.

"Listen," I said, "if this is the future you were talking about, it's pretty cool."

"You think so?" they asked.

"Oh yeah. All this fame, all this money. It's incredible. Like a dream come true."

"Maybe," they said. "But the dream will turn into a nightmare."

"How can you say that?"

"Doing things your way instead of God's is always fun," they said, "but only for a while."

"And then?"

"Then it turns sour. It always gets bad."

"Bad?" I laughed. "If it gets any worse I think I'll die from it being too good."

They looked at me and quietly answered, "You'll wish you could die."

"What do you mean?"

"It's time to transport you fifty years into the future," they said.

"What?"

Without an answer they all raised their hose attachments and shouted, "Ready!"

"Hey, wait a minute," I called.

"Aim!"

"What makes you think I want to leave. I'm happy. Things couldn't go any bett—"

"Fire!"

WOOOOOOSSSSSSSSHHHHHHHhhhhhh . . .

* * * * *

Once again I was falling and tumbling through time.

When I finally landed, I was sitting in a giant chair at the head of a table longer than an airport runway. It looked like we were in the middle of some sort of fancy board meeting. There were dozens of hotshots in expensive suits sitting around nervously looking at me like I was an even hotter hotshot.

At the other end of the table someone was jabbering about the millions of dollars the company would make off a new doll that looked and sounded exactly like—you guessed it, yours truly.

"Not only does it shove up his glasses and eat

Gooey Chewy bars," he was saying, "but it also has a money-back guarantee to fall over, run into something, or create a major disaster every seven and a half seconds."

He wound up the doll and set it on the table. We all watched as it took three steps and crashed on its face, then two steps and stumbled into someone's coffee, then another three steps and fell off the table, shouting a very believable and quite familiar:

"AUGHhhhhh . . ."

I thought it was a pretty good impression, but no one showed any emotion . . . until I grinned.

Then, suddenly, they all grinned.

Then I laughed.

And suddenly they all laughed.

I was about to leap up and run around the room (just to see how far they'd play this Simple Simon Smooch-Up-to-the-Boss Game). But for some reason I couldn't get to my feet.

I glanced down at my body and saw the reason. Besides a Gooey Chewy bar in each hand, I noticed I'd also put on a few pounds. Actually 271. I don't want to say I was fat, but if the Goodyear Blimp ever broke down, they could use me to film all those bowl games.

Suddenly all of the hotshot suits were jumping up and trying to help me to my feet:

"Please, Mr. McDoogle, allow me."

"Let me give you a hand, Mr. McDoogle."

"Oh, Mr. McDoogle, what a lovely tie you're wear—"

"Sit down!" I shouted.

I was amazed at how gruff my voice sounded. I was even more amazed at how everyone ran back to their seats and cowered in terror. Not only had I grown pretty heavy over the last fifty years, but it sounded like I'd gotten pretty mean, too.

I gave up trying to stand just as the doors burst open. A skinny old man in rags staggered into the room. "Mr. McDoogle, Mr. McDoogle," he shouted, "you've got to help us."

I recognized the voice but couldn't place the face. Another old timer limped in behind him. She was in worse shape than he was. She had a pathetically wrinkled face and worn out clothes, but at least I was able to recognize her.

"Wall Street?" I cried in stunned amazement.

"Yes, sir," she said, giving a low bow. "I'm so sorry for the interruption. I told Opera that he couldn't barge in like this, but he—"

"Wait a minute," I said, turning to the skinny old man. "Are you Opera?"

"Of course I am."

"But . . . what happened? How'd you get so skinny?"

"I'm starving to death. Just like everybody else in the country."

I scruntched my eyebrows into a scowl. "But . . . how? . . ."

"You know how!" he shouted. "Ever since you ordered all the world's food to go into making extra Gooey Chewy bars, there's been nothing for the rest of us to eat."

"I . . . I can do that?" I asked.

"Of course you can. You can do anything you want. You're the great Wally McDoogle, the richest and meanest man in the world!"

"I am?" But before I could find out any more good news about myself, we were interrupted by a deafening:

WHOP-WHOP-WHOP-WHOP

We all turned to look out the large window of our towering office building. There was a helicopter hovering just outside.

"Wally McDoogle," a voice bellowed from the helicopter's loud speakers. "This is Billy Buckleman."

"Billy Buckleman?" I turned to Opera. "Is that Billy Buckleman, the great athlete from our school?"

"The great *EX*-athlete," Opera corrected.

"Why ex?"

"Don't you remember?" Wall Street offered. "He fell in that gopher hole during the Little League All-City Championship fifty years ago. He got so discouraged that he quit sports all together."

"That's right," Opera said, inching his way closer to my Gooey Chewys. "The poor guy dropped out of school; turned to a life of crime; and when he came to you for help, you had him arrested."

"I did?"

"Wally McDoogle!" the voice yelled from the helicopter. "I've escaped from prison, and I've come for my revenge. The building is wired to blow up. In just a few seconds I will-ill press this-is-is. . . . Wait a minute. What-at-at's going on-on-on?"

I didn't need anybody to answer that one. I could tell by all the shaking that my old buddy the WUM was dropping by for a little social call. I spun around and sure enough:

K-BLAM!

He was breaking through the wall, just like old times.

Everyone gasped. He had grown even uglier and more menacing than before. I don't want to say he was scary, but if you were to picture your worst nightmare, then picture your worst nightmare having a worst nightmare . . . well, at least you would be getting close.

He wailed mournfully as he turned his giant head (complete with a couple of dozen double chins) back and forth searching the room.

At last he spotted me. With great effort he raised his massive hand to the controls of the motorized chair, shoved the lever forward, and started rolling directly toward me.

His wailing grew louder as he headed toward me faster and faster. And then, just when I was trying to decide whether to let him run over me or beat him to the punch by having a good, old fashioned, heart attack—

> *SNAP* . . .
> > *ZIP* . . .
> > > *FLASH* . . .
> > > > *POP* . . .

Once again everything went into slow motion as my twelve selves showed up in the room with their usual smoke and special effects.

"Am I ever glad to see you guys!" I cried.

"We thought you might be," they said.

I motioned around the room. "I can't believe all this will happen."

"And it's only the beginning."

"How did I get to be so rich, and mean, and . . . plump?"

"It's all tied together," they said. "Your cheating brought you fame, your fame brought you riches, your riches brought you power, and your power brought you incredible greed."

"But, what about the meanness?" I asked.

"The more powerful you got, the meaner and tougher you had to become to hang onto that power. But you've only seen the beginning."

"You're not serious."

"I'm afraid so," they said.

I shook my head in amazement. "All of this for just changing one detail?"

"Every detail counts," they said. "Everything's part of a plan."

I was beginning to get the point.

"Now will you come back with us to repair the damage?" they asked.

I glanced around. There was Opera shouting at me. There was Billy Buckleman blowing me up. There was the WUM running me over. It was like everybody wanted a piece of me. And by my current size it looked like there would be plenty to go around.

Still, I wasn't completely convinced.

"Look," I argued. "Maybe I can change this. Maybe I can turn things around and still keep all the fame and money and stuff. Maybe I could even join a health club."

They shook their heads. "After all this, you still don't want to go back?"

I shrugged. "I don't know."

"We were afraid of that," they said as they re-aimed their vacuum cleaners.

"Hey, what are you doing?"

"Time for one last stop."

"Where am I going now?"

"Another fifty years into the future. Ready!"

"Wait a—"

"Aim!"

"Come on fellows, can't we talk this—"

"Fire!"

WOOOOOOSSSSSSSHHHHHHHhhhhhh . . .

Chapter 9
The Final Chew Down

Once again I was either traveling through time or tumbling inside somebody's blender. It's kinda hard to tell the difference when you're in such pain.

But this time my photocopy buddies made a major mistake. This time they had either transported me underneath some gigantic boulder or under some overfed elephant carrying that boulder. Whatever I was under, it weighed so much I could barely breathe.

"Help . . . me . . ." I gasped. I tried to open my eyes, but the weight was also pressing them down shut. "Get . . . it . . . off. . . ."

"There's nothing on you," my vacuum cleaner pals answered in their usual unison.

"That's . . . im . . . poss . . . ible. . . ."

"Open your eyes, Wally."

"I . . . can't. . . ."

"Yes, you can."

I tried with all of my might. It was like some-body had tied a giant, hundred-pound weight to each lid, then tossed on a couple of armored trucks just for good measure. It took all of my effort, but at last I managed to crack them open just the slightest bit.

What I saw made me wish I hadn't opened them at all.

I was sitting amidst the crumbled ruins of a city. Every building had collapsed. Every wall had caved in and fallen. There was nothing left. Except for one distant room with a closed door, everything had been reduced to piles of rock and rubble.

And the smell. It was worse than my gym locker. There was rotting garbage everywhere.

The place was spooky, big time. The only thing spookier was the sound.

There was none.

Except for the wind that blew and swirled trash in all directions, there was only silence.

"What . . . happened . . . ?" I gasped. "Who . . . did . . . this . . . ?"

"You did," my choir of Wallys answered.

I tried to turn to them, but the weight on me was too great.

"What . . . happened . . . ?"

"You had everybody destroyed."

"What? . . . Why?"

The first Wally swooped down closer and tried

to explain. "The older you got, the more power-ful you became. And like we said before, the more powerful you became, the meaner you grew. You wanted everything your way no matter what. You became a selfish old man, Wally. You hated any-one who crossed you."

"That's . . . not . . . true," I choked.

"I'm afraid it is," he said.

I began to hear another sound—squeaking, lots of it.

"What's . . . that?" I asked.

"Take a closer look."

I squinted my eyes. At first I thought the ground was moving, but it wasn't the ground. It was rats. Millions of rats. I gasped. They were swarming over everything. Squealing and squeaking and swarming.

The first Wally explained. "When all the people were gone, the rats moved in."

"My family? . . ." I gasped. "Wall Street . . . Opera . . . ?"

"All gone."

The words hit like someone had punched me in the gut. "How . . . ?" I stammered.

"Starvation."

"Could . . . I . . . have helped?"

"Sure. But you were too greedy. And there were all those Gooey Chewy bars you had to manu-facture to eat."

This was too much to handle. My head began to spin. I could feel my eyes burn with tears, but I couldn't seem to raise my hands to wipe them.

"What . . . about . . . the WUM?"

He looked at me sadly. "Don't you know yet?"

"Know?"

He gave a pitiful look to the others.

"Tell . . . me . . . ," I demanded.

He motioned to two Wallys who swooped down behind me. Then, ever so slowly, I felt myself being turned. The best I could figure, I was sitting on something with wheels, and they were rotating it around.

I spotted two other Wallys propping up a large, broken mirror. I continued rotating toward the mirror until, at last, I was able to see my reflection.

"NO!" I screamed. "NOOO!!!"

The first Wally sadly nodded. "I'm afraid so."

"IT CAN'T BE!"

"Yes," he said. "Wally Ulysses McDoogle," he pointed first to my reflection then to myself, "meet Wally Ulysses McDoogle. Better known as W.U.M."

I couldn't believe my eyes. It was *me!* I was the WUM. *I* was the monstrous mountain of flesh. WUM wasn't a name. It was initials. *My* initials. W.U.M. *W*ally *U*lysses *M*cDoogle. *I* was the disgusting creature everyone was afraid of. *I* was the wailing, monster of blubber traveling back in time trying to destroy myself. Now all the weight on me made sense. There was nobody on top of me. There was just me. Me in all my terrible tonnage.

"PLEASE," I cried. "NO. . . ."

The first Wally gently explained. "It's you, Wally. The WUM is you. You're the one who's been traveling back in time trying to destroy yourself."

"But . . . why?" I sobbed.

"Because you were so unhappy. You knew if you went back in time and destroyed yourself, you would no longer exist. And no existence would be better than this existence."

Tears ran down my enormous cheeks and off my multiple chins. My heart was breaking. I couldn't stand it. I had to get away. Anywhere.

I remembered the WUM chasing me. I remember how he . . . how *I* had maneuvered the controls of the giant, motorized chair.

The first Wally saw the look in my eyes and cried in alarm, "Wally, no!"

But I had to get away. With great effort I raised my monstrous arm and rested it on the control box.

"Wally!"

Then with all of my strength I pushed the lever.

"Wally, don't!"

But in true McDoogle fashion I shoved the chair into reverse instead of forward and shot backwards just slightly under the speed of sound.

"Wally!" They all raced after me.

I picked up speed.

"Look out!"

Thousands of rats scrambled out of the way as I rolled through the sea of squealing tails and bodies.

Then, as only my McDoogle luck would have it, I realized I was heading toward the one and only building that was still standing.

"No!" they cried. "Not in there!"

The one and only building still standing with a closed door.

K-BAMB!

Well, at least it had been closed.

Now I was plowing through a room darker than Aunt Zelda's roots after a bad hair dye job. All around me were shelves stacked to the ceiling with boxes and—

K-BOOM!

. . . a mighty hard wall at the far end.

I hit that wall with such force that I tumbled off the chair and crashed onto the floor. The impact caused the room to shake violently until the shelves started breaking from their supports and began spilling their boxes on top of me.

"Help!" I cried.

Out of those boxes tumbled dolls. Thousands of wind-up Wally McDoogle dolls. Thousands of wind-up McDoogle dolls all starting to walk and crawl on top of me. All chanting the same thing:

We love you, Wally. You are great.
We love you, Wally. You are great.
We love you, Wally. You are great—

"What's happening?" I screamed.

We love you, Wally. You are great.
We love you, Wally. You are great—

"You programed all the dolls to say that!" the first me cried from outside the door. "They've been your only source of company for years."

We love you, Wally. You are great.
We love you, Wally. You are—

Of course I wanted to jump up and throw them off, but I was too heavy to move.

We love you, Wally—

But that wasn't my only problem. The squeaking of the rats grew louder. I looked up and saw them swarming into the room. They were starved for food, and since I couldn't defend myself, it looked like they were coming at me for a free lunch.

ᵴqueak, ᵴqueak, ᵴqueak . . .

We love you, Wally. You are great.
We love you, Wally.

"Somebody . . . please . . ."

ᵴqueak, ᵴqueak, ᵴqueak . . .

I could feel their wet noses and whiskers as they sniffed my soft skin.
"HELP ME!"
"You've got to go back!" the twelve Wallys shouted. "There's no other way!"

We love you, Wally. You are—
        ᵴqueak, ᵴqueak . . .
great. We love you,—

All of this . . . the destruction of the world, the death of my friends, my hideous self, the rats, the toys . . .

We love you, Wally.
        ᵴqueak

You are—
squeak
We love . . .

all because of one little change.

We
squeak
love
squeak, squeak
you,
squeak . . .

"Make it stop!" I screamed. "Make them stop!"

Wally.
squeak
You
squeak
are—

"You have to go back."

We love.
squeak, squeak
You are—

"Yes!" I cried. "Anything to stop this! Take me back! Take me back!"

We
squeak, squeak, squeak
love you, . . .

"Are you sure?"

squeak, squeak, squeak
You . . .

"YES!" I screamed. "YES!"

. . . are great.
squeak, squeak, squeak . . .

"Ready!" I heard one of me shout.

squeak, squeak, squeak

"Aim!"

We love
squeak, squeak . . .

"FIRE!"
But instead of the ol' familiar WOOSSHhhh . . .
I felt somebody shaking me.
"Wally," a voice was saying, "Wally, are you all right? Wally, wake up. . . ."

Chapter 10

Wrapping Up

I opened my eyes and there was Billy Buckleman staring down at me. "Are you all right?" he asked.

I blinked, trying to figure out where I was. There had been no *Wooosshhhhing,* and no tumbling around in the spin, wash, and dry cycle of some cosmic time machine. One minute I was Wally the econo-sized rat bait. The next I was regular ol' Wally the dork-oid . . . with a king-size headache.

"What happened?" I mumbled.

"The ball, it hit you on the head."

"Ball?" I asked.

"Yeah, you stumbled in that gopher hole over there and the ball bounced right off the top of your head."

"So I'm back at the All-City Championship?" I asked eagerly.

"Of course."

"And I didn't catch the ball?" I asked even more hopefully.

"I'm afraid not."

Now I was practically shouting with enthusiasm. "And we lost?"

"Well, not exactly." He held out his glove and grinned. "It bounced off your head and right into my mitt!"

I stared at the ball not believing my eyes. He had caught it.

"*You* caught the ball?" I asked, sitting up in amazement. "You caught the ball, and *you're* the hero?"

"Well," he shrugged, "I don't know about the hero part, but I caught the ball."

I couldn't believe my ears. "So you're not going to quit sports? You're not going to drop out of school or become a crook or try to blow me up?"

He cocked his head at me in concern. "You sure you're okay?"

I glanced around for my friends in the flying vacuum cleaners, but there was nobody in sight. Just the hundreds of crowd members swarming onto the field. And instead of my name, they were all chanting somebody else's: "Bill-y Bill-y Bill-y."

They joined the rest of the team as they came out and surrounded us, all the time chanting, "Bill-y, Bill-y, Bill-y. . . ."

A moment later they had lifted him onto their shoulders. Coach was right there with them. He was so excited that he almost smiled at me. I smiled back and watched as they carried Billy off the field continuing their chant, "Bill-y, Bill-y, Bill-y. . . ."

"Whay woo woh, Whoaaly!"

I turned around and saw my best friend, Opera, complete with the over-stuffed, chipmunk cheeks and drooling mouth. I was so excited to see him that I threw my arms around him and cried, "Opera, oh Opera, you're alive, you're alive . . . and so fat!"

"Hey," he said between gulps of hot dog number 57, "you don't have to get personal about it."

"Tough break, Wally."

I spun around to see my other best friend, Wall Street.

Of course, I also had to give her my official I'm-glad-you're-still-alive-and-you-look-a-lot-better-without-the-wrinkles hug.

She pushed me back and scowled, "What's wrong with you?"

"It's a long story."

She shook her head. "Too bad about missing that ball. If you would have caught it, you'd have been the hero, and we could have made some really big bucks."

"Maybe," I said, "but maybe there's more to life than being popular and making big bucks."

"Really?" she frowned. "Like what?"

"Like being me."

She looked at me skeptically. "You sure that ball didn't hit you too hard on the head?"

I grinned and turned as the three of us started toward the parking lot. "Seriously," I said, "if I had caught that ball, who would be the president of our Dork-oids Anonymous club?"

She gave me a look.

"Or who would replace me as the Human Walking Disaster Area? . . . Or serve as our All-School Catastrophe? . . . Or—"

I stopped as I spotted a bunch of smoke barreling out of the nearby concession stand.

"Hey, Mister," I shouted. "You all right?"

A tall, skinny guy emerged from the smoke. He was coughing and pushing up a pair of glasses that looked exactly like mine. "It's okay," he said. "My toaster just caught fire."

Something about the glasses and a smoking toaster sent a chill through me.

"Need some help?" Opera asked.

"Naw," he said, waving the smoke aside, "I just short-circuited everything when I plugged this hand-held vacuum into the same outlet."

Suddenly, I felt a double chill.

"Hey," he said, "all the heat melted these Gooey Chewys." He held out an entire box to us. "You guys want them?"

I was growing a little tired of getting all the chills, so I tried something else . . . like running for my life.

"Hey, Wally," Wall Street shouted as I dashed out into the parking lot and down the street as fast as I could. "Wally, where you going?"

I didn't stick around to answer. Of course I was sure it had all been a dream and this was all just a coincidence . . . but I was also sure that I wasn't taking any chances.

"Hey, Wally, come back!"

Whether everything had been a dream or whether it had actually happened really didn't make much difference. The point is I'd learned three very important lessons . . .

— Always let someone else repair my home appliances,
— Start cutting back on my Gooey Chewy intake,
— And let God be God.

* * * * *

Well, it had been quite an adventure with more than my daily minimal requirements of mishaps.

So when I got home I thought I'd relax and turn
on ol' Betsy. I was a little surprised to see that the
Flame Boy story had either been erased or had
never been written.

Hmmm . . .

In any case, it didn't take long to rewrite it. And
once I finished that, I began straining my brain
to come up with an ending. . . .

When we last left our wannabe hero,
he had successfully spread his flames
across the entire sky. A neat trick to
stop Arctic Guy's attempt to turn Earth
into a giant Popsicle, a lousy way to
ruin this year's school clothes.

But there is still one minor problem...the 734 nuclear missiles the
President had fired at the giant blob
of Sunscreen #85. The good news is they
will wipe out the Sunscreen. The bad
news is they will also wipe out any and
all life upon the planet.

There is a burst of superhero music
as Flame Boy suddenly has a major hot
flash. He curls up into another fireball and this time hurdles himself
toward the Sunscreen. It's going to be

close. (It has to be, since this is the climax of the story.) But if he can wrap his flames around the Sunscreen and evaporate it before the missiles arrive, then they'll pass right through it and head into outer space where they won't harm anybody...(unless you count that giant fleet of UFO's coming to invade us, but that should probably be left for another story).

Flame Boy arrives and quickly surrounds the Sunscreen, just as Arctic Guy throws open the door to his orbiting refrigerator and shouts, "Hey, what's all the racket?"

"I'd love to explain," Flame Boy answers, "but right now, I'm kinda tied up saving the world." With that he turns back to the Sunscreen and flames up for all he is worth. The music grows louder as the missiles close in.

The Sunscreen begins to evaporate.

The music grows even louder as the missiles really close in.

The Sunscreen continues evaporating.

The music grows even louder as the missiles really, really close in.

But, try as he might, Flame Boy can't

get hot enough to evaporate all of the
Sunscreen. And then, just when you're
thinking, "I knew a superhero made out
of flame was kinda lame," Arctic Guy
has an idea of his own.

He takes a deep breath and blasts out
a blustery blow. Although his breath
is as bad as in the previous sections
of this story (he's still eating those
garlic and clam sauce toppings on his
onion-flavored yogurts) his wind fans
up Flame Boy's flames. Our hero begins
heating hotter and hotter. The
Sunscreen evaporates faster and faster.

Meanwhile the music is growing really
loud and the missiles are really,
really, really closing in. Really.

With a final burst of energy, Flame
Boy evaporates the last of the
Sunscreen...just as the missiles pass
through on their way to blow up that
UFO fleet we're not supposed to talk
about.

"You did it!" Arctic Guy shouts.

Flame Boy leans back and wipes the
sweat from his forehead (a neat trick
for someone made of flames). "No," our
hero sighs, "we did it."

"You're right!" Arctic Guy beams. "*We* did! We make quite a team, don't we? You with your flames, and me with my cold."

"Hey, maybe we could go into business together or something?" Flame Boy suggests.

"But I thought you wanted to be a superhero."

"Nah, I'm not really cut out for it. Besides, who wants to put up with all of that noisy superhero music? Actually, I just want to be the best me I can be. Nothing more, nothing less."

"I know what you mean," Arctic Guy agrees. "I never really wanted to be the world's vilest villain, either."

"What'd you want to be?"

"I always wanted to own a pizza parlor."

"Hey, I got a keen idea," Flame Boy says. "Let's open up a pizza parlor together. I could cook the pizzas, and you could freeze them."

"Wow, that's hot," Arctic Guy cries.

"Not only is it hot, it's cool," Flame Boy says. "And I know just who our first customer will be."

"Who's that?"

"The President. In fact he's still waiting for his deluxe pizzas with extra cheese and anchovies."

And so the two head off into the sunset. Dreaming their dreams, sharing their—

"Hey, can you lower your flames just a little?" Artic Guy asks. "You're melting my face."

"Oh sorry," Flame Boy answers. "Say, would you mind chewing on these breath mints? You're making my eyes water."

"No problem. I'm all for bettering myself."

"Me, too."

And so the world is once again a cooler, safer, and better-smelling place to live, as the two friends stop trying to be something they aren't and decide to be the best of who they are.

I looked at the ending and smiled. Sounds like we were all learning a few lessons.

But all this talk about food was making me hungry. So I shut off ol' Betsy and headed down the stairs to heat up, what else but, a frozen pizza.

Not of course without tripping over Collision the cat, tumbling down the steps and crashing into an end table, which of course knocked over the lamp, which momentarily set our house on fire.

Yes sir, it was nice to know things were definitely getting back to normal.

About the Author

Bill Myers is the author and co-creator of the best-selling "McGee and Me!" book and video series, which has sold 2 million episodes and has appeared several times as ABC's Weekend Special. He has written over three dozen books, and his work as a film maker has earned over 40 national and international awards. When he's not roaming the world making movies, he enjoys speaking at conferences and working with the youth of his local church. Bill lives in California with his wife, Brenda, and their two children.

You'll want to read them all.

THE INCREDIBLE WORLDS OF WALLY McDOOGLE

#1—My Life As a Smashed Burrito with Extra Hot Sauce

Twelve-year-old Wally—"The walking disaster area"—is forced to stand up to Camp Wahkah Wahkah's number one all-American bad guy. One hilarious mishap follows another until, fighting together for their very lives, Wally learns the need for even his worst enemy to receive Jesus Christ. (ISBN 0–8499–3402–8)

#2—My Life As Alien Monster Bait

"Hollyweird" comes to Middletown! Wally's a superstar! A movie company has chosen our hero to be eaten by their mechanical "Mutant from Mars!" It's a close race as to which will consume Wally first—the disaster-plagued special effects "monster" or his own out-of-control pride . . . until he learns the cost of true friendship and of God's command for humility. (ISBN 0–8499–3403–6)

#3—My Life As a Broken Bungee Cord

A hot-air balloon race! What could be more fun? Then again, we're talking about Wally McDoogle, the "Human Catastrophe." Calamity builds on calamity until, with his life on the line, Wally learns what it means to FULLY put his trust in God. (ISBN 0–8499–3404–4)

#4—My Life As Crocodile Junk Food

Wally visits missionary friends in the South American rain forest. Here he stumbles onto a whole new set of impossible predicaments . . . until he understands the need and joy of sharing Jesus Christ with others.
(ISBN 0–8499–3405–2)

#5—My Life As Dinosaur Dental Floss

It starts with a practical joke that snowballs into near disaster. Risking his life to protect his country, Wally is pursued by a SWAT team, bungling terrorists, photo-snapping tourists, Gary the Gorilla, and a TV news reporter. After prehistoric-size mishaps and a talk with the President, Wally learns that maybe honesty really is the best policy. (ISBN 0–8499–3537–7)

#6—My Life As a Torpedo Test Target

Wally uncovers the mysterious secrets of a sunken submarine. As dreams of fame and glory increase, so do the famous McDoogle mishaps. Besides hostile sea creatures, hostile pirates, and hostile Wally McDoogle clumsiness, there is the war against his own greed and selfishness. It isn't until Wally finds himself on a wild ride atop a misguided torpedo that he realizes the source of true greatness. (ISBN 0–8499–3538–5)

#7—My Life As a Human Hockey Puck

Look out . . . Wally McDoogle turns athlete! Jealousy and envy drive Wally from one hilarious calamity to another until, as the team's mascot, he learns humility while suddenly being thrown in to play goalie for the Middletown Super Chickens! (ISBN 0–8499–3601–2)

#8—My Life As an Afterthought Astronaut

"Just cause I didn't follow the rules doesn't make it my fault that the Space Shuttle almost crashed. Well, okay, maybe it was sort of my fault. But not the part when Pilot O'Brien was spacewalking and I accidently knocked him halfway to Jupiter. . . ." So begins another hilarious Wally McDoogle MISadventure as our boy blunder stows aboard the Space Shuttle and learns the importance of: Obeying the Rules!
(ISBN 0–8499–3602–0)

#9—My Life As Reindeer Road Kill

Santa on an out-of-control four wheeler? Electrical Rudolph on the rampage? Nothing unusual, just Wally McDoogle doing some last-minute Christmas shopping . . . FOR GOD! Our boy blunder dreams that an angel has invited him to a birthday party for Jesus. Chaos and comedy follow as he turns the town upside down looking for the perfect gift, until he finally bumbles his way into the real reason for the Season. (ISBN 0–8499–3866–x)

#10—My Life As a Toasted Time Traveler

Wally travels back from the future to warn himself of an upcoming accident. But before he knows it, there are more Wallys running around than even Wally himself can handle. Catastrophes reach an all-time high as Wally tries to out-think God and re-write history. (ISBN 0–8499–3867–8)

Look for this humorous fiction series
at your local Christian bookstore.